Shopkins™

Once you shop...You can't stop!

SUPERMARKET SURPRISES

ISBN 978-0-545-90500-8

10 9 8 7 6 5 4 3 2   15 16 17 18 19

Printed in the U.S.A.   132

First printing, September 2015

SCHOLASTIC INC.

AT THE SUPERMARKET!

What surprises are in store at Small Mart? Use the stickers to fill in the scene. Are Kooky Cookie and Le'Quorice having a silly conversation? Maybe Lolli Poppins and Miss Mushy-Moo are planning an aisle-hopping party!

2

ADVENTURE IN EVERY AISLE

Each group of Shopkins has an aisle in the Small Mart that they call home. Use the colored number stickers to match the Shopkins to their correct aisles.

Miss Mushy-Moo

Posh Pear

Corny Cob

Pineapple Crush

Yo-Chi

Freezy Peazy

Popsi Cool

Spilt Milk

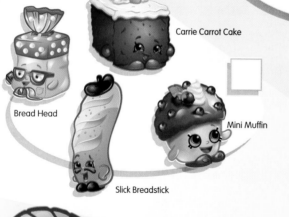

Carrie Carrot Cake

Bread Head

Mini Muffin

Slick Breadstick

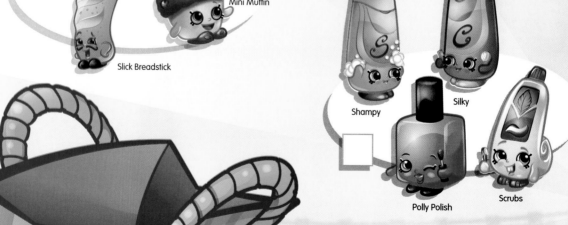

Shampy

Silky

Polly Polish

Scrubs

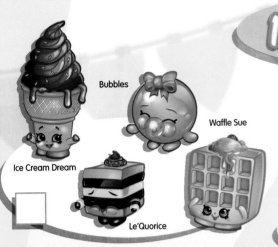

Bubbles

Waffle Sue

Ice Cream Dream

Le'Quorice

1. FRUIT AND VEG

2. PANTRY

3. DAIRY AND FROZEN FOOD

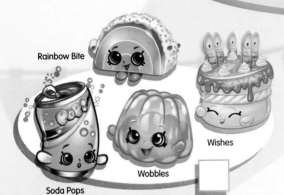

Rainbow Bite

Wishes

Soda Pops

Wobbles

4. SWEET TREATS

5. BAKERY

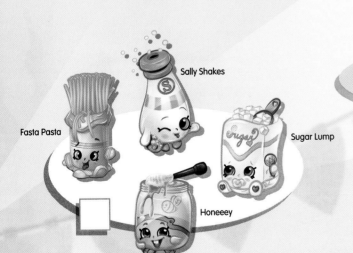

Sally Shakes

Fasta Pasta

Sugar Lump

Honeeey

6. HEALTH AND BEAUTY

7. PARTY FOOD

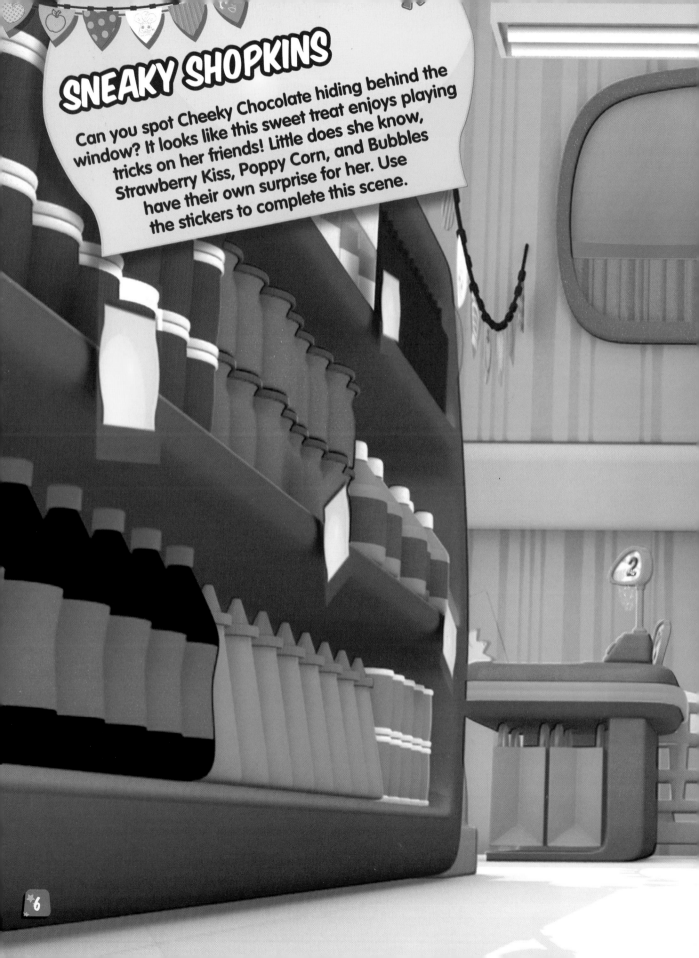

SNEAKY SHOPKINS

Can you spot Cheeky Chocolate hiding behind the window? It looks like this sweet treat enjoys playing tricks on her friends! Little does she know, Strawberry Kiss, Poppy Corn, and Bubbles have their own surprise for her. Use the stickers to complete this scene.

6

PUZZLE PERFECTION

The Shopkins are counting on you to fill in the missing pieces of the puzzle below! Use the stickers to complete the image of Yo-Chi and her friends.

Once You Shop... You Can't Stop!

8

SMALL MART MAZE

Oh, no! Spilt Milk slipped down the wrong aisle and can't find Wishes. Complete the maze to reunite the two friends. Then place the sticker of Wishes on top of her picture.

CHECKOUT DANCE-OFF!

The Shopkins are having a dance-off! Toasty Pop and Pineapple Crush show off their sweet moves while Dum Mee Mee cheers them on. Will Apple Blossom and Cheeky Chocolate come up with their own dance number? Use the stickers to see who wins this off-the-cart contest!

SHOPKINS SUDOKU

Use the stickers of Chee Zee, D'lish Donut, and Lippy Lips to complete the Sudoku puzzle below. Remember . . . each column and row shouldn't contain more than one of each character!

12

TIC-TAC-TOE

Challenge a friend to a game of tic-tac-toe! Use the stickers of Juicy Orange and Sneaky Wedge to play. Each player gets to choose a Shopkins. One at a time, take turns placing a sticker on the grid. To win the game, you must get three of your stickers on the same line.

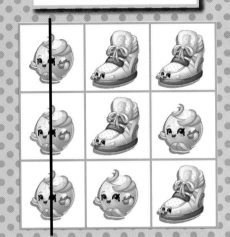

GAME 1

GAME 2

GAME 3

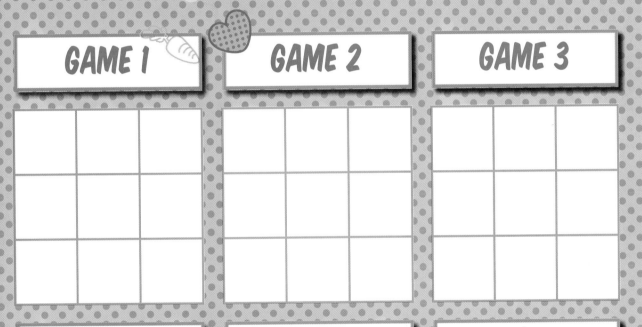

GAME 4

GAME 5

GAME 6

WHICH COOKIE IS KOOKY?

One of these images of Kooky Cookie has an extra chocolate chip than the others. Find and circle it. Don't be fooled—Kooky is a master of disguise! Circle only the image of Kooky with an extra chocolate chip.

PICTURE PERFECT

Apple Blossom loves looking her berry best! Use the grid below to draw her pretty portrait and then color it in.

ANSWERS

Pages 4-5

Page 9

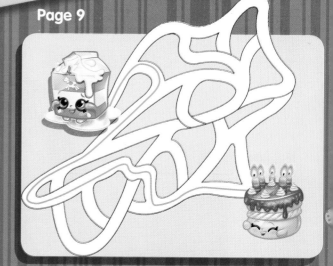

Page 12

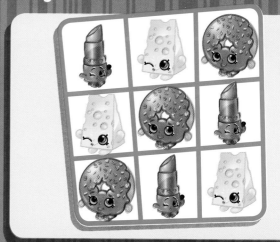

Page 14

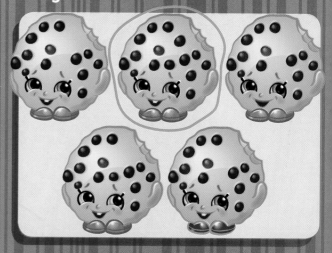

CHECK YA LATER!

Stickers for pages 2-3

Stickers for pages 4-5

1 2 3
4 5 6
7

Stickers for pages 6-7

Stickers for pages 10-11

Stickers for page 8

Sticker for page 9

Stickers for page 12

Stickers for page 13

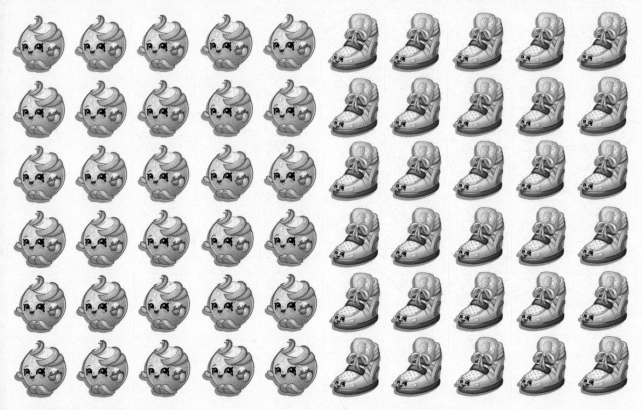

Make Up Your Own Small Mart Signs!

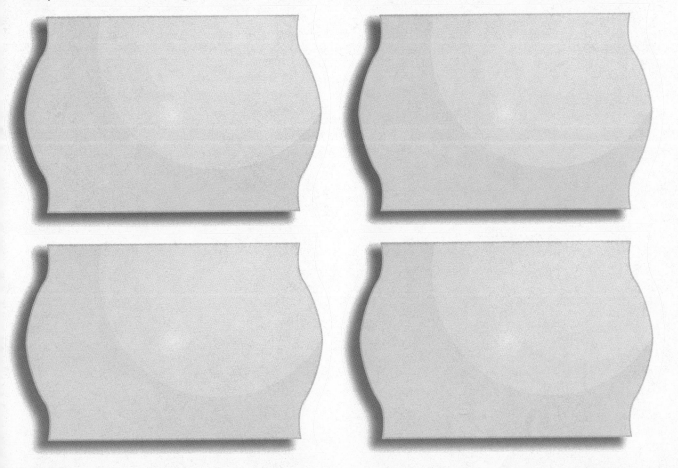